BENTLY & egg

Story and Pictures by

WILLIAM JOYCE

A LAURA GERINGER BOOK

AN IMPRINT OF HARPERCOLLINS PUBLISHERS

Bently & egg

Copyright © 1992 by William Joyce

Printed in the U.S.A. All rights reserved.

Library of Congress Cataloging-in-Publication Data

Joyce, William.

Bently & egg / William Joyce.

p.   cm.

"A Laura Geringer book."

Summary: A shy, singing frog is left in charge of a very special
egg that changes his life.

ISBN 0-06-020385-4. — ISBN 0-06-020386-2 (lib. bdg.)

[1. Frogs—Fiction.   2. Ducks—Fiction.   3. Eggs—Fiction.]
I. Title.

PZ7.J857Be 1992   91-55499

[E]—dc20   CIP

                                                          AC

Typography by Christine Kettner

1 2 3 4 5 6 7 8 9 10

First Edition

For Franny Baucum,
who is *nothing* like a frog.
W. J.

BENTLY HOPPERTON was a young and rather musical frog who loved to draw. Whenever he felt extremely happy, he would burst into song. His best friend was Kack Kack, a recently widowed duck-of-the-wood who lived next door. She took care of Bently. She made sure his clothes were clean, nursed him when he was sick, and loved his songs and drawings.

"Oh, sing to me, Bently," she'd say, and happy in the company of his one true friend, Bently would sing his heart out. But one day Kack Kack forgot to ask Bently to sing, and she forgot to look at his drawings. In fact, she forgot Bently altogether. At sunset Bently went looking for Kack Kack and found her sitting very quietly on her nest.

"Look, Bently!" she said proudly, rising. There, in the middle of the nest, was a single white egg.

"Isn't it beautiful?" asked Kack Kack.

Bently didn't know. "It's just an egg," he thought.

Kack Kack spent all her time sitting on her beloved egg. Bently was lonely. "I haven't a friend in the world," he said sadly to himself.

One day Kack Kack received a message by cricket courier: Her sister had just hatched seven little ducklings. "Oh, Bently, I must go and see them. Would you please watch over my egg while I'm gone?"

"Well ... okay," he said.

"Thanks—you're such a dear," she quacked, and pecked him on the cheek.

Left alone with the egg, Bently frowned. "Silly old egg," he muttered. Soon one wood creature after another scurried by the nest.

"We're off to see the new ducklings," they said. "Won't you come with us, Bently?" But Bently shook his head and sat glumly guarding Kack Kack's solitary egg.

Bently stared at the egg. He didn't know why, but he just didn't like it. It looked bald and bare. It looked dull and pale. It looked *so* blank. Then he had an idea. He would paint the egg!

He did a beautiful job, a masterful and extraordinary job. The egg looked dazzling. Never in the history of the wood had there been such a special egg. "Now this is an egg a frog could get attached to," said Bently proudly, then pulled out his banjo and began to sing.

> *"Oh, special egg, oh, roundy egg,*
> *Oh, splendid, artful Bently egg,*
> *I painted you with feelings too*
> *Mysterious to say to you."*

Bently felt happy beyond words.

Suddenly there was a great rustling. Tree limbs crackled. Shouts echoed. There was a boy in the woods!

"Oh, my goodness, better hide!" said Bently, and he tried desperately to cover the egg with straw and leaves, but it was too late.

A hand reached into the nest and roughly grabbed the egg.

"Smash!" said the boy, raising it above his head. But then he looked at its remarkable decoration. And he looked again, more closely.

"The Easter Bunny left it," he whispered in awe.

"Easter Bunny, my eye," thought Bently. "That's a Bently Hopperton egg!"

The boy cradled the egg carefully in his hands and ran away. Bently was beside himself. "Eggnapped!" he cried. "I'll save you, egg. Don't worry, egg. Armed only with my wits, I'll not fail you, egg," he vowed bravely, and took off in pursuit.

"Oh, please let him be careful with my egg," Bently pleaded aloud as he hopped desperately through the underbrush. But Bently could not keep up. As he came out of the wood and into the vegetable garden, he found to his horror that the boy was nowhere in sight.

"Oh, heavens, I'm lost!" he moaned.

"Me too," sighed a stuffed elephant standing next to a row of cabbages. "I've been out here a week! I think they forgot me. I hope it doesn't rain."

"Oh, dear, so do I," said Bently with genuine concern. "Did a boy carrying an extraordinary egg pass by here?"

"Yep," said the elephant. "He turned left at the cucumber squash; he never even noticed me."

"Thanks so much," said Bently as he dashed away. "Don't worry. I'll try to send you help."

"Appreciate it," said the elephant.

At the cucumber squash, Bently found the tracks of the boy's bare feet and followed them through the garden and into the house. He had never been in a house before, so he was more than a little afraid.

"I must not falter. The egg is all," he whispered to himself to bolster his courage.

Going from room to room, Bently finally spotted the egg on top of a table.

Using a nearby balloon, Bently floated up to the egg. Deftly lassoing it, he quickly examined it for cracks. It was still perfect! His decoration was perfect too—not even a smudge.

"Oh, joy! Oh, rapture!" he sighed, then broke into song:

"Oh, foundling egg, my captured egg . . ."

"There's really no time for a serenade, you know," interrupted the watery voice of a nearby goldfish. "He'll be back any second."

"You're right," said Bently, embarrassed. "I just get carried away sometimes!"

"Don't we all," sighed the goldfish.

Then, using all his might, Bently loaded the egg into the basket of the balloon; but before he went aloft, he scribbled a message for the boy:

The egg is mine. It needs me. Your elephant is in the garden. It needs you.

Bently Hopperton

"You won't tell him which way we went, will you?" Bently asked the goldfish.

"Cross my gills and hope to drown."

"Thanks," said Bently, and he and the egg floated toward the window.

To Bently's dismay, the balloon drifted back down the hall and into the room of a little girl who sat propped up in her bed, painting. She looked a bit like the boy only nicer.

"Hello there," said the girl. "Do you like my pajamas? They're new."

"Very lovely," replied Bently.

"I'm sick, you know. The Easter egg hunt is today and I'm going to miss it," said the girl with a sigh.

"Oh, I'm sorry," said Bently.

"That's a nice egg you've got there!" said the girl. "A *really* nice egg."

"Why, thank you," said Bently, tightening his grip on the egg. "I'd give it to you, but it belongs to someone else."

"Oh, I see. No eggs for me, I guess," said the girl, shaking her head sadly.

"Look here!" said Bently impatiently, for he thought Kack Kack might be home by now and worrying. "I've got an idea." In a flash, he painted an egg on a piece of paper, which he handed to the little girl. She smiled. The egg matched her pajamas.

Bently hopped back into the balloon, and the little girl, smiling sweetly, gave it a gentle shove.

"Thanks," Bently called as they sailed out the window.

The breeze was steady; the balloon flew straight and true. Never had frog or egg soared so high. Bently was moved to song:

> *"Oh, flying egg, sky-highing egg,*
> *My aeronautic high-up egg,*
> *I look at you as we drift through*
> *The heavens that are bright and—"*

But before Bently could finish, there was a loud hissing and the balloon began to plummet to the ground. Bently looked up. There was a hole in the balloon! Bently looked down. There was an Easter egg hunt just below them. They were headed straight for a lady in a great big hat.

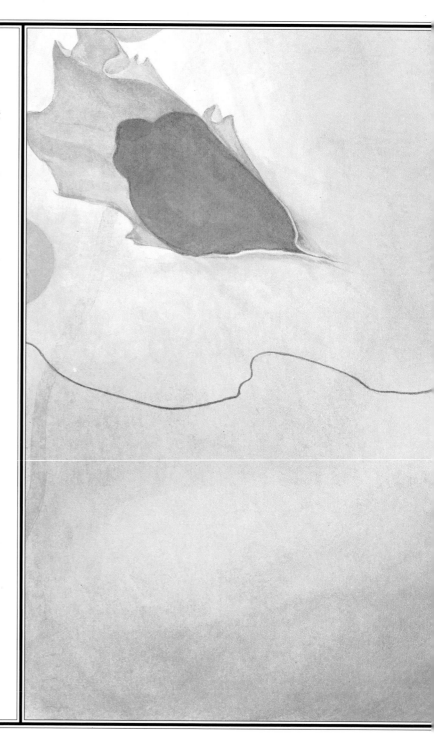

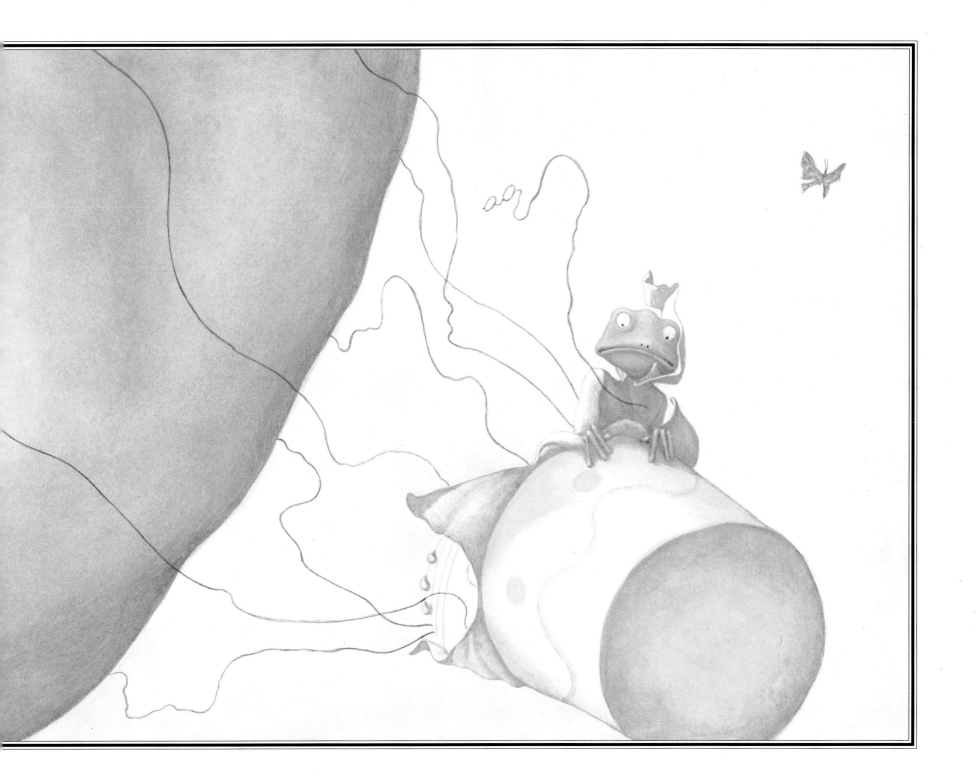

Bently shut his eyes and clutched the egg for dear life. The balloon smacked onto the woman's head, and Bently and the egg spilled out onto her hat.

"Daphne! Daphne! There's a frog on your hat!" someone screamed.

Bently grabbed the egg and, trying to look nonchalant, hopped to another woman's hat. The lady next to her began to scream. Everybody began to scream. Food began to fly. There was pandemonium!

Amid all the confusion, Bently and the egg, disguised as hors d'oeuvres, slipped away undetected.

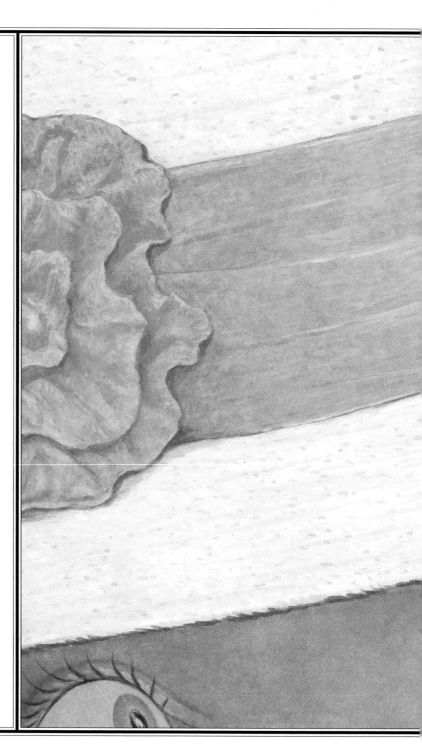

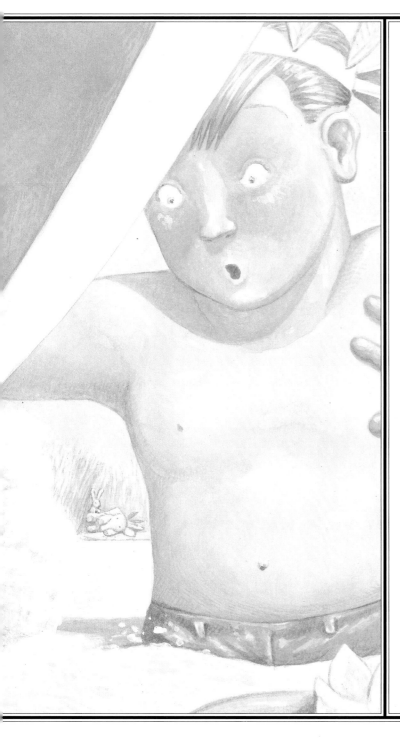

Leaving the party in ruins, Bently spotted a toy boat moored to the bank of a pond. "I'm sure no one would mind if we borrowed this for a bit," he said, panting. Wearily, he loaded the egg on board and cast off.

"Something of a sea dog, aren't I?" said Bently to the egg, and with a flourish he took the ship's wheel and steered a course across the pond.

The egg sat amidships shimmering in the afternoon sun. It looked beautiful. Once again Bently was moved to song:

> *"Oh, sailin' egg, mast-mainin' egg,*
> *Our travels have been whirligig.*
> *I sail us to your mother, who*
> *Sits at home and yearns for—"*

But once again events would not let him finish, for straight ahead, wading toward them, was the boy.

"I want my egg back," he demanded, and threw a rock, which smashed against the ship's bow.

"I have not yet begun to fight!" Bently proclaimed, and fired the ship's cannons.

The roar of the guns so startled the boy that he ran off crying for his mother.

"Smart bit of sailoring, if I say so myself," Bently said to the egg with some pride. Then he noticed the ship was sinking.

"Aaaah!" cried Bently, exasperated. There was no time to lose. He cut away a line of the ship's rigging, tying one end to his waist and the other around the egg. He swam desperately to shore. The egg was very heavy and almost pulled him under several times. He was soon tired, but paddled valiantly on. Finally with his last remaining ounce of strength, Bently plopped the egg upon the shore and whispered hoarsely, "Silly old egg, safe at last." Then he laid down his head and fell into a deep, exhausted sleep.

Bently hadn't noticed, but the egg had been washed clean. All his beautiful decorations were gone. But even if he had noticed, he would no longer have cared, for now he loved the egg just the way it was.

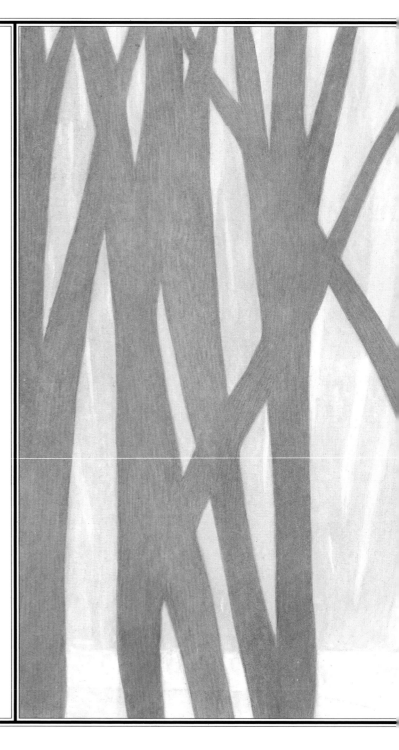

It was a long time before Bently woke up. He blinked his eyes and looked over at the egg. His heart sank. It was broken, covered with a dozen tiny cracks.

"Oh, no . . . oh, no . . . " he moaned.

Then the cracks grew wider and wider, and he heard a tiny sound. It was the sound only newborn ducklings make. The shell began to crumble, and out wobbled the most beautiful baby duck Bently had ever seen.

Then he saw that Kack Kack was there. "It's a boy! It's a baby boy!" she cried, and gently smoothed the duckling's downy feathers.

Suddenly, there was a great hue and cry. "Hooray for Bently. Long live Bently!" Startled, Bently looked around. It seemed every creature in the wood was there—bugs, birds, squirrels.

"I think I'll name him Ben, after you," said Kack Kack, helping Bently to his feet. "It's the least I can do, with all you've done."

"All I've done? How did you find out?"

"Well, a goldfish told a gnat, and the gnat told some of us," said a turtle. "And a little girl told a butterfly, and the butterfly told most of us," said a wren.

"And an elephant told a rabbit, and the rabbit told all of us," said a squirrel.

"It seems you have quite a few friends now," said Kack Kack. "I'm so proud of you, Bently."

Bently blushed and smiled modestly.

The next afternoon, when everything was quiet again, Kack Kack said, "Oh, sing to us, Bently." And Bently, happy in the company of his two best friends, sang his heart out.

"Oh, happy you, oh, happy me.
The three of us will always be
The best of friends through thick and thin—
Bently, Kack, and little Ben."

And they were all, each one, happy beyond words.

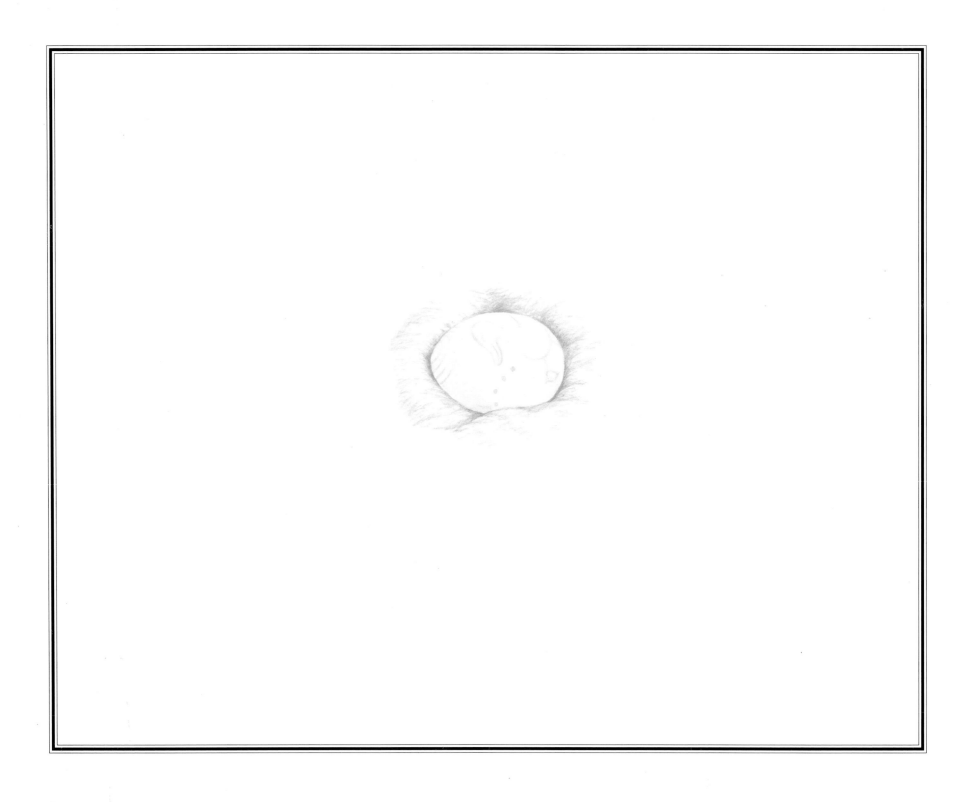